231628

F

or b

THIS BOOK BELONGS TO:

D0487120

Other Kipper books

Kipper
Kipper's Toybox
Kipper's Birthday
Kipper's Snowy Day
Where, Oh Where, is Kipper's Bear?
Kipper's Book of Colours
Kipper's Book of Opposites
Kipper's Book of Counting
Kipper's Book of Weather

Honk!

Mick Inkpen

FALKIRK COUNCIL
LIBRARY SUPPORT
FOR SCHOOLS

h

*Hodder
Children's
Books*

A division of Hodder Headline plc

'Honk!' said the gosling.

'Where did you come from?' said Kipper.

'Honk!' said the gosling again.

'You can go in the
      bath!' said Kipper.
   'Honk!' said the gosling
to the plastic duck,
which didn't reply.

'Do you like
bubble bath?'
said Kipper.
  'Honk!' said the gosling,
blowing a bubble
  by accident.

'Can you only say
Honk!' said Kipper.
The gosling nodded.
And honked again.

It honked
at the towel.
It honked
at the sponge.
It honked
at the hairdryer. . .

E specially when
it blew him
out of the bathroom!

A nd it honked
as it bumped
into Big Owl!
'Are you all right?'
said Kipper.

But the gosling
didn't reply.
It didn't say 'honk'.
It fell fast asleep,
without saying
anything at all!

FALKIRK COUNCIL
LIBRARY SUPPORT
FOR SCHOOLS

FALKIRK COUNCIL
LIBRARY SUPPORT
FOR SCHOOLS

First published 1998
by Hodder Children's Books,
a division of Hodder Headline plc,
338 Euston Road, London NW1 3BH

Copyright © Mick Inkpen 1998

10 9 8 7 6 5 4 3 2 1

ISBN 0 340 71631 2

A catalogue record for this book
is available from the British Library.
The right of Mick Inkpen to be identitfied
as the author of this work
has been asserted by him.

All rights reserved

Printed in Italy